CARSTENSZ PYRAMID

Tamra B. Orr

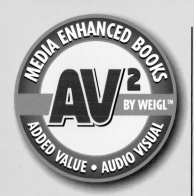

AV² provides enriched content that supplements and complements this book. Weigl's AV² books strive to create inspired learning and engage young minds in a total learning experience.

Your AV² Media Enhanced books come alive with...

Audio
Listen to sections of the book read aloud.

Key Words
Study vocabulary, and complete a matching word activity.

Video
Watch informative video clips.

Quizzes
Test your knowledge.

Embedded Weblinks
Gain additional information for research.

Slideshow
View images and captions, and prepare a presentation.

Try This!
Complete activities and hands-on experiments.

... and much, much more!

Go to **www.av2books.com**, and enter this book's unique code.

BOOK CODE

AVY56934

AV² by Weigl brings you media enhanced books that support active learning.

Published by AV² by Weigl
350 5th Avenue, 59th Floor
New York, NY 10118
Website: www.av2books.com

Library of Congress Cataloging-in-Publication Data
Names: Orr, Tamra, author.
Title: Carstensz Pyramid / Tamra B. Orr.
Description: New York : AV2 by Weigl, [2019] | Series: Seven summits | Includes index. | Audience: Grade 4 to 6.
Identifiers: LCCN 2019009586 (print) | LCCN 2019017854 (ebook) | ISBN 9781791114176 (multi User ebook) |
ISBN 9781791114183 (single User ebook) | ISBN 9781791114152 (hardcover : alk. paper) | ISBN 9781791114169
(softcover : alk. paper)
Subjects: LCSH: Jaya, Mount (Indonesia)--Juvenile literature. | Natural history--Indonesia--Jaya, Mount--Juvenile literature. | Mountain ecology--Indonesia--Jaya, Mount--Juvenile literature.
Classification: LCC GB545.I65 (ebook) | LCC GB545.I65 O77 2019 (print) | DDC 995.1/6--dc23
LC record available at https://lccn.loc.gov/2019009586

Printed in Guangzhou, China
1 2 3 4 5 6 7 8 9 0 23 22 21 20 19

052019
102318

Editor: Katie Gillespie
Designers: Tammy West and Ana Maria Vidal

Every reasonable effort has been made to trace ownership and to obtain permission to reprint copyright material. The publishers would be pleased to have any errors or omissions brought to their attention so that they may be corrected in subsequent printings.

Photo Credits
Weigl acknowledges Getty Images, Alamy, iStock, Dreamstime, and Shutterstock as its primary photo suppliers for this title.

CARSTENSZ PYRAMID

SEVEN SUMMITS

CONTENTS

A Contrast in Color

Hidden by the clouds and fog of the central highlands of Papua province, Indonesia, is Carstensz Pyramid. Also called Puncak Jaya, it is one of the highest peaks in the world. Rising 16,024 feet (4,884 meters) above sea level, Carstensz Pyramid is very difficult to climb.

Carstensz Pyramid is made largely of limestone. The rocky mountain has a year-round crown of snow and ice, despite the fact that it is only a few degrees from the **equator**. This snow is a stark contrast to the dense green rainforests far below.

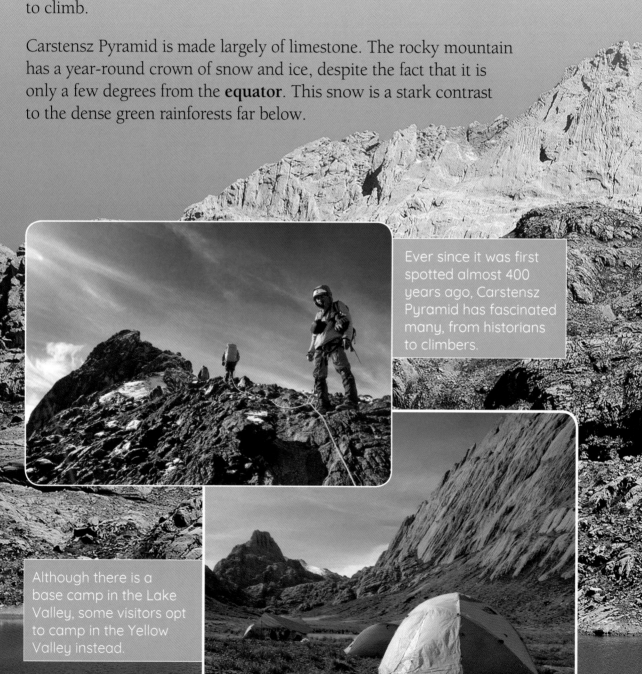

Ever since it was first spotted almost 400 years ago, Carstensz Pyramid has fascinated many, from historians to climbers.

Although there is a base camp in the Lake Valley, some visitors opt to camp in the Yellow Valley instead.

MAP OF CARSTENSZ PYRAMID

Pacific Ocean

INDONESIA

★ **Carstensz Pyramid**

Papua New Guinea

Australia

LEGEND

☐ Water

☐ Land

☐ Indonesia

★ Carstensz Pyramid

N W E S

MAP SCALE

0   400 MI / 400 KM

CARSTENSZ PYRAMID FACTS

- Carstensz Pyramid is called by many different names. Some indigenous peoples refer to it as *Dugundugu*, or "Ice," while others call it *Namangkawee*, or "White Arrow."

- The name *Puncak Jaya* means "Summit of Victory."

- While some climbers hike to the base of the mountain, many others take an expensive helicopter ride to base camp instead.

- Climbers must often rope walk from one peak to another to keep moving up the mountain.

A Remote Mountain

Carstensz Pyramid is located on the island of New Guinea, the second-largest island on Earth. New Guinea is split into two parts. The country of Papua New Guinea is on the east side. On the west side of the island are the Indonesian provinces of West Papua and Papua. Carstensz Pyramid is part of the Sudirman mountain range in the province of Papua.

The closest settlement to Carstensz Pyramid is the city of Timika. It is only 38 miles (61 km) from the mountain's base. This is where most climbers travel to before starting their journey up the mountain.

Papua New Guinea is made up of more than 600 small islands in the southwestern Pacific Ocean.

Most of the Papuan population is Christian.

Puzzler

Glaciers are found on every continent in the world except Australia. Usually, they are located where the weather is cold. Using an atlas or the internet, research what percentage of the world's glaciers are found in each of the following places. Then, match each percentage to the correct location.

LOCATION
1. Antarctica
2. Greenland
3. North America
4. Asia
5. South America/
   Europe/Africa/
   New Zealand/Papua

PERCENTAGE OF EARTH'S GLACIERS
A. Less than 0.5 percent
B. 0.2 percent
C. 91 percent
D. Less than 0.1 percent
E. 8 percent

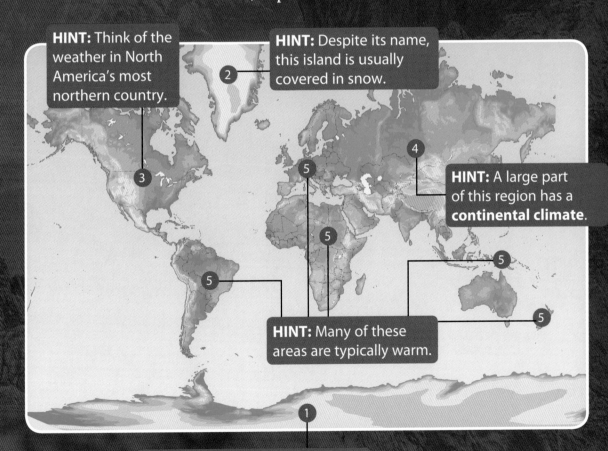

HINT: Think of the weather in North America's most northern country.

HINT: Despite its name, this island is usually covered in snow.

HINT: A large part of this region has a **continental climate**.

HINT: Many of these areas are typically warm.

HINT: The weather here is always cold, and people are rarely found, except for scientists.

A: 1.C 2.E 3.A 4.B 5.D

Plates on the Move

The Maoke Mountains are located in the province of Papua. They are made up of two ranges. In the east is the Jayawijaya Range and in the west is the Sudirman Range. Carstensz Pyramid is the highest peak in the Sudirman Range.

The Sudirman Range is named after one of Indonesia's greatest heroes and military leaders, Raden Sudirman. It is thousands of years old. The range was formed by the collision of **tectonic plates**.

One plate was moving north from Australia, while another was moving northwest from the Pacific. Over time, hot **magma** from under the ground pushed up, forcing itself into layers of rock and creating the mountains. The process also created the Grasberg gold and copper mine, one of Carstensz Pyramid's most valued sites.

The Sudirman Range has a total of four peaks. These are Sumantri, Ngga Pulu, Carstensz East, and Carstensz Pyramid.

Gold and Copper

In 1936, Dutch mountain climber and geologist Jean Jacques Dozy was exploring Carstensz Pyramid. During his trip, he spotted an outcrop of rocks with green streaks. He took a few samples from the rocks back to base with him. When he had them tested, they turned out to be rich in gold and copper deposits.

It did not take long for Dutch investors to find the Grasberg mine, 14,000 feet (4,267 m) up in the Sudirman Mountains. For about 40 years, millions of dollars in gold and copper were excavated. Just when it seemed like these valuable minerals had run out, a company called Freeport found more. Today, the Grasberg mine is considered the largest and richest gold mine in the entire world. Experts estimate that the mine's reserves are worth more than $100 billion.

It takes thousands of employees to run the mine. To support them, Freeport has built houses and schools, as well as an airport, a hospital, and even an aerial tramway.

Fog Forests and Primeval Forests

Since the peak of Carstensz Pyramid is covered in ice and snow all year, nothing is able to grow in its cold temperatures and frigid winds. The first **vegetation** does not appear until dropping down to 11,480 feet (3,500 m). There, the first trees grow in an area sometimes called "the fog forest." These trees are barely surviving, often stunted and crooked, and covered in clumps of moss.

Travel down to 9,800 feet (3,000 m), and the mountain begins to blossom with bright green ferns and their curly leaves, as well as pale orchids with waxy leaves. Much of this area is known as a primeval forest. It is largely untouched by humans.

From 6,500 feet (1,980 m) down to 3,000 feet (914 m), a new world emerges, filled with lush flowers, bushes, plants, and trees. Carstensz Pyramid's base is surrounded by thick rainforests. These feature more than 1,300 species of trees and 2,770 species of orchids. The lowest area around the mountain is made up of freshwater swamps where sago palm trees and swamp grass grow thick and strong.

Three-quarters of Papua is covered in forests.

Outstanding Orchids

New Guinea is known for its wide variety of orchids. Environmental groups such as the World Wildlife Fund have continued to find new species of this delicate flower throughout the island. **Botanist** Wayne Harris, a leading authority on such plants, has called the area a "goldmine of orchids."

Orchids are not just beautiful to look at. Certain species are added to recipes, while others are ingredients in perfumes or tea blends. In some parts of the world, orchids are even used for medicinal purposes. Some people believe that orchids can help treat colds or improve a person's eyesight.

More than 10 percent of the world's orchids are found in New Guinea.

From Echidnas to Wallabies

The area around Carstensz Pyramid is home to 190 species of **mammals**, including cuscuses, echidnas, wallabies, and tree kangaroos. The cuscus, a cousin to the possum, is about 18 inches (45 centimeters) long. During the day, it sleeps in trees. At night, it hunts for leaves and fruit, as well as for small birds and reptiles. It uses its long tail and sharp claws to help it climb trees and move from one branch to another.

The echidna is a very unusual creature. Also known as the spiny anteater, it is a mammal that lays eggs. The only animals that do this are the long- and short-beaked echidna, and the duck-billed platypus.

Usually growing to only about 3 feet (1 m) tall, wallabies look like smaller versions of regular kangaroos. They are **marsupials**, and can jump high and run fast. Tree kangaroos are also marsupials, but they do not hop around on the ground. Instead, they live in trees, often jumping from one tree to the next. They use their long tails for balancing on tree limbs.

Wallabies and tree kangaroos both have strong legs, as well as pouches for their babies to grow inside.

A World of Birds

New Guinea is well known for its amazing bird species. The cassowary, for instance, is a huge, flightless bird. It has a helmet-like crest on its head, and can change the color of its neck and head based on its mood.

Parrots and cockatoos fly through the island skies, making their homes in the rainforests. They come in a variety of colors, with feathers that are bright purple, blue, green, or red. Cockatoos screech and scream, sending loud messages through the greenery.

New Guinea is especially known for its birds of paradise. There are three dozen different kinds on the island. They show off their vibrant colors, and often have long, wild tails.

Cassowaries often grow to about 6 feet (2 m) tall.

An Unbelievable Sight

When Dutch explorer and **seafarer** Jan Carstensz first spotted a huge mountain in New Guinea, he thought he had to be imagining it. Since he was in a tropical rainforest close to the equator, he did not believe he had actually seen snow. However, Carstensz's 1623 discovery turned out to be correct.

When Carstensz returned to the Netherlands and reported what he had seen, no one believed him. It was not until 1909 that people realized he was right. Another Dutch explorer, Hendrik Albert Lorentz, went to the area and found the mountain. It was named in honor of Carstensz.

Even though the mountain had been found and named, it had not yet been climbed. That changed in 1962. Austrian mountaineer Heinrich Harrer, along with Philip Temple, Russell Kippax, and Albertus Huizenga, reached the peak for the first time.

The year before his Carstensz Pyramid expedition, Harrer practiced mountain climbing on the Dover Heights in Sydney, Australia.

Biography
Heinrich Harrer (1912–2006)

Heinrich Harrer was born in Austria in 1912. Although he was a professional skier, mountain climbing became his real passion. In 1938, Harrer and a team reached the summit of the Eiger Mountain in Switzerland. During the climb, they were almost swept off the side of the White Spider, a vertical wall of ice, by a sudden **avalanche**.

Harrer had a number of other adventures before climbing Carstensz Pyramid. He escaped from a prisoner-of-war camp, crossed the Himalaya Mountains to get to Tibet, and became a friend of famed religious leader, the **Dalai Lama**. Harrer wrote multiple books about his life, one of which was made into the 1997 film, *Seven Years in Tibet*.

Brad Pitt played Harrer in the film version of *Seven Years in Tibet*. He won a Rembrandt Audience Award for Best Actor for his performance.

The Impact of Climate Change

As the world warms up due to climate change, glaciers such as those found on Carstensz Pyramid are melting. Already, glaciers in the mountain's Meren Valley and at Puncak Trikora have disappeared. This can result in higher sea levels, flooding, and a lack of fresh drinking water. Climate change puts many other areas of the world at risk as well.

North America

South America

Atlantic Ocean

Pacific Ocean

Glacier National Park, Montana (melting glaciers)

Amazon Rainforest, South America (drought/deforestation)

LEGEND
- Water
- Land
- Antarctica

N
W E
S

MAP SCALE
0
2,000 MI
2,000 KM

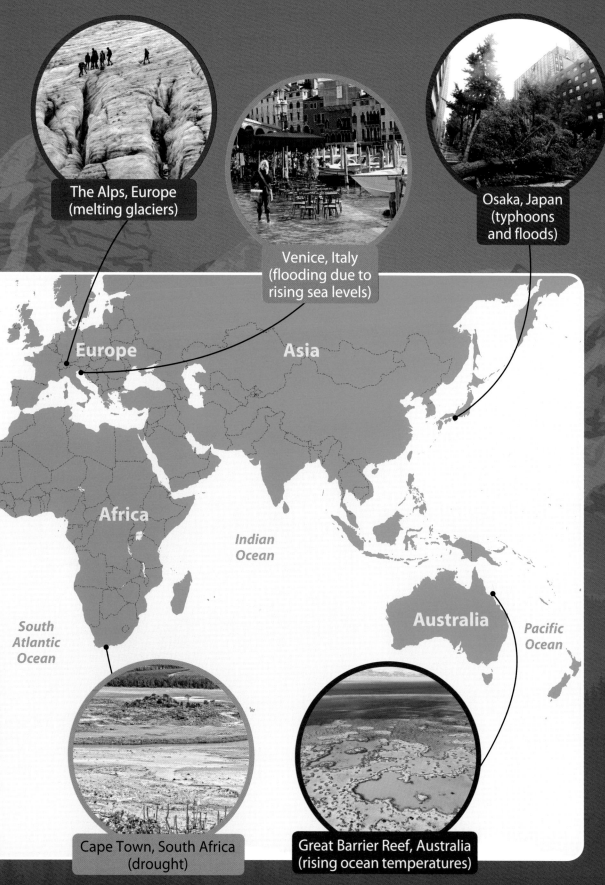

The Alps, Europe
(melting glaciers)

Venice, Italy
(flooding due to
rising sea levels)

Osaka, Japan
(typhoons
and floods)

Europe

Asia

Africa

Indian
Ocean

South
Atlantic
Ocean

Australia

Pacific
Ocean

Cape Town, South Africa
(drought)

Great Barrier Reef, Australia
(rising ocean temperatures)

Around the Mountain

Although no one lives on Carstensz Pyramid, a number of indigenous groups live in the northeast highlands and the southern jungle. The Dani people are found in the highlands' Baliem Valley. Until Dutch explorers found them in the 1930s, this group of hunter-gatherers lived simply, with no metal tools. They were written about as "stone-age people."

By the early 1950s, Christian **missionaries** arrived. Others followed, and over time, the people in this area changed. However, they still wear traditional clothing with decorations made from feathers, shells, and bones. Today, they happily share their culture with the visitors and climbers who travel through the valley.

The Damal people live in the jungle. Like the Dani, their lives changed when they were first found in the 1930s, and Dozy discovered gold in Carstensz Pyramid. As more people came to the area, the Damal found themselves pushed out of their homes, so many moved to the coast.

The Dani participate in an annual event called the Baliem Valley Festival. It features mock battles to symbolize the high spirit and power that have been practiced for generations.

A Land of Languages

The entire country of Papua New Guinea is only about the same size as the state of California. About 8.5 million people live there, compared to California's 39.5 million. Despite this, Papua New Guinea boasts an impressive record.

At more than 800, Papua New Guinea has the highest number of spoken languages on Earth. Some languages are only spoken by a few dozen people, while others have thousands of speakers. Of its many languages, three are official. These are English, Hiri Motu, and Tok Pisin.

Hiri Motu was first spoken by Motu people around Port Moresby, the capital of Papua New Guinea. It has now spread to inland plantations and trade centers.

Carstensz Pyramid Timeline

8,000 YEARS AGO

Prehistoric

50,000 years ago The first settlers arrive in New Guinea.

About 11,700 years ago Earth's last **Ice Age** ends.

8,000 years ago New Guinea becomes separated from Australia.

ABOUT 11,700 YEARS AGO

Exploration

1623 Dutch explorer Jan Carstensz first spots what will become known as Carstensz Pyramid.

1909 The mountain is reached by a group of Dutch explorers.

1623

1920 Dutch explorers find some of the first indigenous peoples living around the mountain.

1936 The first copper deposits are found in mountain glaciers in Indonesia.

1920

Development

1962 Carstensz is successfully climbed for the first time.

1962–1969 The New York Agreement gives control of West New Guinea to the United Nations. It is transferred to Indonesia the following year, but not officially taken over until 1969.

1962–1969

1967
The Indonesian government signs over rights to extract minerals from the Grasberg mine to the Freeport company.

1988

1988 Freeport discovers far more gold and copper ore deposits at the Grasberg mine.

1995 The mountain is officially closed to climbers and tourists.

Present

1994–2000 The Meren Glacier largely disappears.

2005 The mountain is reopened to climbers and tourists.

2014 The Indonesia Women **Seven Summits** team reaches the mountain's summit. While there, the team replaces climbing ropes.

2014

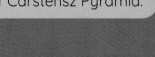
2005

2018 Two men successfully fly in a tandem paraglider from the side of Carstensz Pyramid.

Key Issue: The Grasberg Mine

The Grasberg mine has helped support the local economy. It has also produced thousands of jobs for people in the area. However, there has been a great deal of debate about whether the mine is helping or hurting the people and the environment of Papua.

Thousands of Papuans work at the mine, but they are not the only ones who are hired there. Over time, the company that owns the mine has been bringing in outsiders to work at Grasberg instead. This has upset many people in nearby communities.

It has been reported that the Grasberg mine dumps tens of millions of tons (tonnes) of mine waste, or tailings, directly into the Aikwa River system. It has been doing this for decades. This practice has turned thousands of acres (hectares) of forest into a wasteland.

According to some accounts, on a good day, panners can find up to 0.1 ounces (3 grams) of gold.

Due to violence and tension in the area, the mine and its workers are protected by armed security guards.

Since so much waste is dumped into the Aikwa River, countless Papuans line up on either side of the water with their own pans and supplies. Some spend each day panning for gold, in the hopes of giving their children better lives and educations. They sell anything they find to local buyers.

SHOULD THE GRASBERG MINE CONTINUE TO STAY OPEN?

YES	NO
It provides jobs for 19,500 people.	Not all of the jobs are being filled by local residents.
It has reserves worth more than $100 billion.	Mine waste has been dumped over large areas of forests, destroying any growth.
It gives some people the chance to pan for gold and sell it to local buyers.	The sediment from the mine is killing animal and fish species, and polluting the rivers. Some fear it will also pollute groundwater used for drinking.

Determination and Patience

All over the world, there are people who see a mountain and are inspired to climb it. Each year, at least 30,000 people attempt to climb Mount Kilimanjaro, the world's highest free-standing mountain. When it comes to Carstensz Pyramid, however, only a few hundred have actually made it to the top. It takes enormous endurance just to get to the base of the mountain, as well as enough patience and money to get the proper permits, and excellent climbing skills to reach the summit.

Reaching the mountain's base often means a four to six day trek through the humid rainforest. Everyone must turn in their climbing schedules or itineraries to the police before starting their trip. Climbers need to have permits in place as well, as the number of people allowed has been controlled since the mountain reopened in 2005.

The Papuan government does not always make this process easy for applicants. Also, the area is considered to be unstable. A number of wars between different groups can make Papua a risky place to visit.

Flying to the base by helicopter instead of hiking cuts days off the journey.

A Tough Climb

Carstensz Pyramid is the only one of the world's Seven Summits that requires technical or more advanced climbing skills. Once the trip up the mountain begins, it becomes obvious why this is the case. There are steep rock walls, giant ledges, and gaps that can only be covered by balancing carefully on ropes.

Due to its location near the equator, the mountain can be climbed year round. However, this does not mean that weather is not a problem. At base camp, it can be warm and sunny, but it is not unusual to run into rain, ice, and snow on the ascent. Temperatures at the base can range from almost 100°Fahrenheit (38°Celsius) during the day to 14°F (−10°C) at night, depending on the time of year. The higher climbers go, the windier it gets, as well.

Carstensz Pyramid is the highest island peak in the world.

Ready to Go?

Despite the difficulties, a number of climbers have traveled to Carstensz Pyramid to attempt to reach its peak. Each one has been faced with challenges that require strong muscles and bravery. For example, in one spot, climbers must get across a 50-foot (15-m) gap. To do this, they use the Tyrolean traverse maneuver, which requires them to pull their bodies upside down along a suspended steel cable.

The equipment needed to undertake a climb like this includes harnesses, **carabineers**, and jumars, or rope clips. Layers of warm clothing are especially important, since it can get bitterly cold as people climb. Most climbers wear several layers, plus special lined boots. A thick pair of gloves is necessary on Carstensz Pyramid because of the sharp limestone rocks.

Trekking poles are also required gear for a journey to Carstensz Pyramid.

What to Expect

Climbers almost always bring guides along on the trip. Although these guides tend to be local, they work for western companies. Using guides is one of the best ways to stay safe, since they know the mountain well. They also know what to do if any equipment fails or if someone is injured during the climb.

The cost to climb Carstensz Pyramid ranges quite a bit, depending on what climbers prefer. The fees are typically $26,000 or more, especially if a helicopter ride is included. This does not include the cost of flights to and from Indonesia, health insurance, or any personal expenses.

The actual climb to Carstensz Pyramid's summit takes climbers about five hours. The descent takes just as long, although it often involves a great deal of **rappelling** to get back down to the ground. A round trip on the mountain takes an average of 11 hours.

Visitors to Carstensz Pyramid will experience a wide range of ecosystems. The area is home to more than half of Indonesia's plant and animal species.

What Have You Learned?

True or False?

Decide whether the following statements are true or false. If the statement is false, make it true.

1 The Grasberg mine produces gold and iron ore.

2 Some cultures use orchids for medicinal purposes.

3 The mountain was shut down for more than 20 years to climbers and tourists.

4 Carstensz is one of the most frequently climbed mountains in the world.

5 Climbers often find the weather on the mountain to be hot and sunny all day.

6 Panning can help local people support their families.

ANSWERS

1. False. The Grasberg mine produces gold and copper ore. **2.** True. Some people believe that orchids can help treat colds or improve a person's eyesight. **3.** False. The mountain was shut down for 10 years to climbers and tourists. **4.** False. It is one of the least climbed mountains. **5.** False. When climbing the mountain, it is not unusual to run into sunshine, rain, snow, and wind. **6.** True. Panners sell anything they find to local buyers.

Short Answer

Answer the following questions using information from the book.

1. Why have so few people climbed Carstensz Pyramid?
2. Who was Jean Jacques Dozy?
3. What is unusual about the short- and long-beaked echidna?
4. Why did people disbelieve Jan Carstensz when he described the mountain he had seen in New Guinea?
5. How does the Grasberg mine affect local wildlife?

Multiple Choice

Choose the best answer for the following questions.

1. What is a primeval forest?
   a. A forest that no one has ever seen
   b. A forest that struggles to grow and survive
   c. A forest that is untouched by humans

2. Which of the following regions of the world is being threatened by drought?
   a. Glacier National Park, Montana
   b. Cape Town, South Africa
   c. Venice, Italy

3. How many people does the Grasberg mine employ?
   a. 19,500
   b. 20,500
   c. 21,500

4. What does the name *Puncak Jaya* mean?
   a. Snowy Mountain
   b. Summit of Victory
   c. Dutch Explorer

Activity

Create Your Own Rainforest

To reach Carstensz Pyramid, climbers and visitors usually make their way through the rainforests surrounding the mountain. Rainforests are full of green trees, bushes, and countless other plants. They grow thick and strong, due to all of the moisture in the area. Try making your own rainforest and see what you can learn about this unusual ecosystem.

Materials

A large aquarium with a lid

Smallgravel

Paper and pen or pencil

Potting soil

A spray bottle of water

Charcoal

Tropical plants

Instructions

1. Put some gravel and charcoal in the bottom of the aquarium. Add enough potting soil to cover the bottom of the aquarium in a layer about 1 inch (2.5 cm) thick. Dampen it with water from the spray bottle.

2. Place the plants in the soil and make sure their roots are covered. Spritz them with water from the spray bottle.

3. Put the lid on the aquarium. Place your rainforest in a warm, well-lit spot.

4. Record any changes you see. Check your rainforest several hours later. Why is there water on the underside of the glass? How is your rainforest like a real rainforest?

5. Check your rainforest a week later. Does the soil still feel moist? Why or why not? If the water evaporated, where did it go?

Key Words

avalanche: a sudden downhill fall of snow

botanist: plant scientist

carabineers: strong metal hooks that connect pieces of equipment

continental climate: a climate that is relatively dry, with hot summers and cold winters

Dalai Lama: the spiritual leader of Tibetan Buddhism

equator: the imaginary line that runs east to west around the widest part of Earth, dividing it in two

Ice Age: a period when Earth was covered with glaciers

magma: molten rock beneath Earth's crust

mammals: warm-blooded vertebrate animals that have hair or fur, and nourish their young with milk

marsupials: animals with a pouch for developing their young

missionaries: followers of a religion who introduce their religion to those in other countries

rappelling: descending by rope

seafarer: someone who travels by sea

Seven Summits: the highest mountains on each of the seven continents

tectonic plates: segments of Earth's crust

vegetation: the types of plants that are found in a specific area

Index

Log on to www.av2books.com

AV² by Weigl brings you media enhanced books that support active learning. Go to www.av2books.com, and enter the special code found on page 2 of this book. You will gain access to enriched and enhanced content that supplements and complements this book. Content includes video, audio, weblinks, quizzes, a slideshow, and activities.

AV² Online Navigation

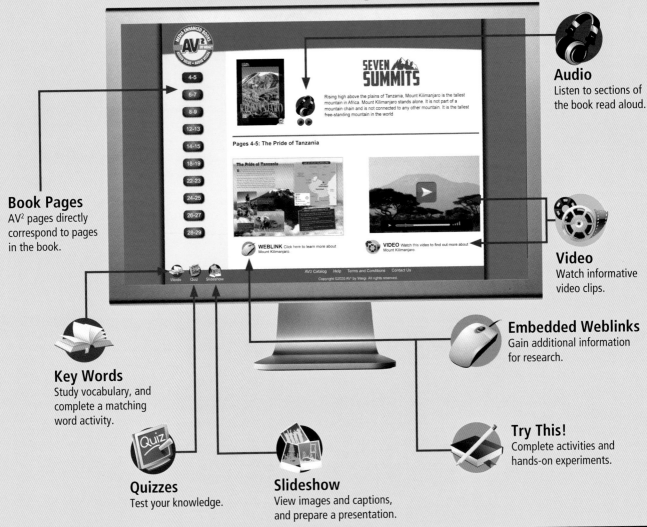

Audio
Listen to sections of the book read aloud.

Book Pages
AV² pages directly correspond to pages in the book.

Video
Watch informative video clips.

Key Words
Study vocabulary, and complete a matching word activity.

Embedded Weblinks
Gain additional information for research.

Try This!
Complete activities and hands-on experiments.

Quizzes
Test your knowledge.

Slideshow
View images and captions, and prepare a presentation.

AV² was built to bridge the gap between print and digital. We encourage you to tell us what you like and what you want to see in the future.

Sign up to be an AV² Ambassador at www.av2books.com/ambassador.

Due to the dynamic nature of the internet, some of the URLs and activities provided as part of AV² by Weigl may have changed or ceased to exist. AV² by Weigl accepts no responsibility for any such changes. All media enhanced books are regularly monitored to update addresses and sites in a timely manner. Contact AV² by Weigl at 1-866-649-3445 or av2books@weigl.com with any questions, comments, or feedback.